W9-BSI-506

# The Beggar and the Bluebird

Anthony DeStefano

Illustrated by Richard Cowdrey

*New York Times Bestselling Artist*

SOPHIA INSTITUTE PRESS
Manchester, NH

*This book is dedicated to my goddaughter, Greenlee, whose singing heart brings joy wherever she flies.*

**— Anthony DeStefano**

*Thanks to Ira, Renee, Henry, and Sylvia!*

**— Richard Cowdrey**

**FROM THE BIBLE:**

*"For I was hungry and you gave me something to eat, I was thirsty and you gave me something to drink, I was a stranger and you invited me in, I needed clothes and you clothed me, I was sick and you looked after me, I was in prison and you came to visit me. . . . Truly I tell you, whatever you did for one of the least of these brothers and sisters of mine, you did for me."*

**— Matthew 25:35–36, 40 (NIV)**

SOPHIA
INSTITUTE PRESS



Printed in the United States of America.

Sophia Institute Press®
Box 5284, Manchester, NH 03108
1-800-888-9344

www.SophiaInstitute.com
Sophia Institute Press® is a registered trademark of Sophia Institute.



ISBN: 978-1-64413-510-5
Library of Congress Control Number: 2021944514

First printing

Once upon a time, there was a bluebird who lived in the city. Like most birds, he flew south every winter to avoid the freezing weather. But one year, he had so much fun soaring above the big buildings and swooping down through the streets that he lost track of time and left much later in the season than he should have. It was already Christmas Eve, and the bluebird knew the first winter snowstorm was about to blow through.

Just before the bird departed, though, he flew down into the park to eat some birdseed that was thrown by a poor beggar.

The beggar was sitting on a bench as he tossed the seeds onto a dirt pathway. He had crutches and seemed like a nice man, so the bluebird started talking to him. He told him that he was flying south for the winter so he could enjoy the warm sunshine and sing all day long. The beggar looked at him and smiled. Then he asked the bluebird to do him a small favor.

"Little bird," he said, "there's a homeless man I know on the other side of the city. He hasn't eaten for days and is very hungry. I have a loaf of bread that was given to me by a kind person this morning. I can't walk very well with these crutches. Will you please deliver the bread to him so he has something to eat?"

"But I can't," the bluebird responded. "I have to fly south for the winter. It's already getting cold, and I can't survive the first frost."

But the beggar persisted. "Please do me this favor. The old man is starving and needs help. If you don't give him this food, he may get very sick."

So the bluebird agreed. He flew off with the bread to the other side of the city and thought: “I hope this won’t take too long.” When he finally found the homeless man, he dropped the loaf of bread into his lap.

"It's a miracle!" the man cried out, as he began to hungrily eat the bread that had fallen from the sky.

When the bluebird returned to the beggar, he told him how happy the old man was. He was about to set off for the South when the beggar asked him another question.

“Little bird,” he said, “there’s a young widow I know who lives in a small, shabby house nearby. She has two children, and she’s very poor. I have a few dollars that were just given to me. Can you bring them to this woman? She needs the money more than I do.”

“Oh, but I can’t,” the bluebird replied. “It’s getting very cold now, and the sky is looking frosty. I simply *must* leave for the South.” But once again the beggar told the bluebird how much the young woman needed help. And once again the bluebird agreed.

So off he flew to the house where the widow lived
and tapped on her door with his wings.

When the woman opened the door, the bird dropped the money into her hands and flew away. The poor lady couldn't believe it.

"This must be a gift from Heaven!" she cried. "Now I can buy a Christmas present for my children!"

The bluebird flew back to the beggar and told him he had given the widow the money. “But now I really have to go,” he said. “I simply *must* fly south.” He could feel the frost beginning to form on his wings and could see that a storm was moving into the city. Once again, though, the beggar pleaded with him to do one final favor.

“I know a sick boy in a hospital a few blocks away,” he told the bird. “And he has just about given up hope. He thinks everyone has abandoned him.”

The beggar pulled a small gold cross from his pocket. “This was given to me long ago,” he said. “If you bring it to the boy, it might make him understand that he’s not alone — that God loves him.”

But this time the bluebird insisted that he could not make the delivery. “Don’t you see, it’s already starting to snow?” he cried. “And if I don’t leave this second, I’m going to get caught in the storm and freeze!”

“But this won’t take long,” the beggar assured him. “And it will bring so much comfort to the little boy. Please help him.”

The bluebird was frightened, but he was sorry for the child. “No one should feel alone, especially at Christmas,” he thought. “And maybe I can fly extra fast.”

So flapping his wings as swiftly as he could,
the bird flew like a shot through the sky.

When he arrived at the hospital, he could see the boy sitting on his bed, alone and sad. He tapped on the window with his beak. The boy looked over, curiously. The winter storm had begun, and the bird was already covered in snow.

The boy opened the window, and the bird carefully placed the cross in his hand. The boy didn't understand, but he realized that the bird was giving him something very special.

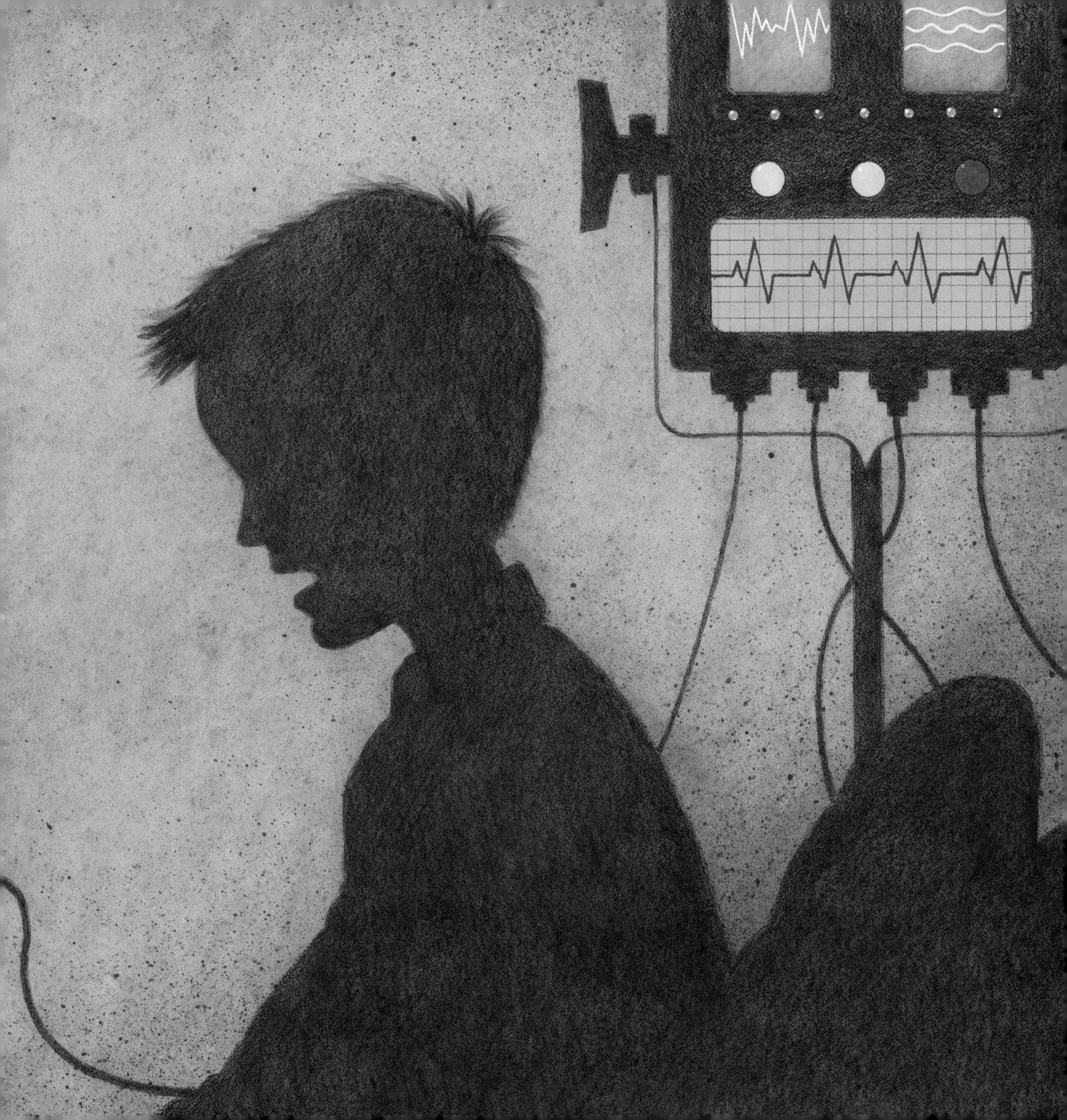

As the bird flew off the ledge, the boy smiled at him, amazed at the gift he had received.

By now the bluebird was very tired. He struggled to fly back to the beggar through the driving snow — which had now become a blizzard — but he was so weak he could barely keep his eyes open. When he finally landed on the ground next to the beggar, he closed his wings tightly around his little body in an attempt to keep out the icy wind.

But it didn't do any good. He was freezing and exhausted. He knew now that he would never see the South. The beggar looked at him with love. "Are you sorry that you stayed to help those poor people?" he asked.

The bluebird thought for a second. "No," he answered, shivering. "I'm glad I was able to make them happy at Christmas. But now I just have to go to sleep."

Then the bird closed his eyes and lay flat and still on the cold ground.

The beggar looked down at him and said: "Little bird, you were willing to sacrifice yourself in order to give others the gift of hope. But you will not die."

The beggar stood up and dropped his crutches. His old, tattered coat slipped to the ground. Then, one by one, the pieces of dark, dirty clothing began to fall from his body.

He started to grow larger, and suddenly, two huge white wings sprouted from his back, and a dazzling white light began to shine ’round his face.

The beggar was not a beggar at all — but an angel.

The angel picked up the bluebird, cupping him softly in his hands. He looked at him and said: “You will never die but will sing your song forever.”

Then the angel spread his wings and leaped into the air, flying upward, through the snow.

Soon they were high above the clouds. The sun was shining brightly, and the angel flew toward it. The bluebird, who had been sleeping, felt the light from the sun on his face and woke up. He was amazed to see how beautiful the sunlit sky looked. "It's so warm," he whispered. "I must be in the South."

Then the angel released him, and the bluebird flew into the sunshine, singing and happily flapping his wings.